The Teeny Weeny Genie

Written by

JULIA DONALDSON

Illustrated by

ANNA CURREY

Old Macdonald had a farm,

And on that farm he had a farmhouse,

And in that farmhouse he had a cupboard,

And in that cupboard he had a teapot,

And in that teapot lived
a teeny weeny blue genie.

The genie liked it in the teapot,
and Old Macdonald didn't like tea,
so life was nice and peaceful.

That is, until the day when Old Macdonald
decided to clean out his cupboard.
"I'll give this dusty old teapot a wash," he said.

And when he started
to rub it dry, the genie
wafted out of the spout.

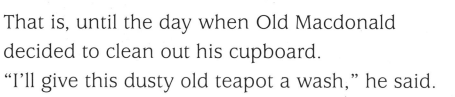

"What is your wish?"
asked the genie.

"Could you manage a new
tractor?" asked the farmer.
"My old one's awfully rusty."

The genie puffed
himself up and said,
"ABC and XYZ,
Gobbledegook and
garlic bread."

He rubbed his tummy
and patted his head, and . . .

. . . a bright red tractor appeared.

"Thank you! Let's go for a ride round the farm!" said Old Macdonald, so they did.

It was a very loud tractor –

Chugga chugga, vroom vroom!

The farm was very noisy too.

Quack quack!

Baa baa!

Moo moo!

The genie blocked his ears.

"This farm is a lot of work," said the farmer. "I wish I had a wife to help me."

The genie puffed himself up and said,
"ABC and XYZ,
Cauliflower cheese and chocolate spread."

He rubbed his tummy and patted his head, and a woman appeared. She was carrying a large suitcase.

"Hello, husband!" she said.
"I'm Mrs Macdonald."

After a quick cuddle and a tractor ride,
Old Macdonald asked, "What's in that suitcase?"
"All my clothes," said Mrs Macdonald. "I wish I had some
wood and a saw and a drill and a hammer and nails.
Then I could build a wardrobe to keep them in."

The genie puffed himself up and said,
"ABC and XYZ,
Gooseberry green and raspberry red."
He rubbed his tummy and patted his head,
and the wood and tools appeared.

Mrs Macdonald set to work.
The saw and the drill and the
hammer were very loud.

whirr whirr!
Eee eee!

Bang bang!

The genie blocked his ears again.

"There's some wood left over," said Mrs Macdonald, and she made a cradle. Then they wished for a baby to put in it.

The baby was very loud too.

Waa waa
waa!

Mrs Macdonald wished for a rattle but that just made the baby cry even louder.

"I think he's wishing for a dog," said the genie.

No sooner had the
dog appeared than
he wished for a bone.

The bone was nice and quiet . . .

but then the dog
wished for a cat
to chase.

The cat ran away from the dog and climbed up a tree.

"She's stuck!" said Old Macdonald, and he wished for some firefighters to come and rescue her.

They appeared in a very loud fire engine.

Nee-nah!

Nee-nah!

Nee-nah!

Nee-nah!

One of the firemen climbed up a ladder to rescue the cat,
while the others stood around wishing for things.

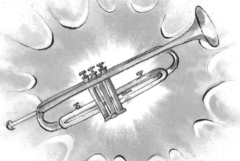

They wished for a trumpet,
an electric guitar
and a drum kit.

"Let's have a band practice," they said.
It was a very loud band practice.

Toot Toot!

Thrum-de-thrum!

Thump thump!

The genie was getting a terrible headache.

As soon as the cat was down from the tree,
she wished for some mice. The mice wished
for a ball and a very loud whistle.

Pheep
pheep!

They all started to play football – until the mouse who was the ref got fed up with that and wished to be Supermouse instead.

Then the cat wished to be Supercat, the dog wished to be Superdog, the Macdonalds wished to be Superfarmers, the firefighters wished to be Superfirefighters, the baby wished to be Superbaby, and they all flew around bumping into each other.

Whizz whizz!

Bang!

Crash!

"I can't stand this a minute longer,"
said the genie. "I wish they'd all go away."

But nothing happened, and then the genie remembered:
"I'm not allowed to make wishes for myself – only for other people."
Hoping that no one was looking, he slunk back into the farmhouse.

"Perhaps they'll leave me in peace if I get back into my dear old teapot," he said.

He stroked the teapot fondly, and then got the surprise
of his life, when out of the spout wafted another genie!
This one was green.

"What were you doing in my teapot?" asked the blue genie.
"Trying to get some peace and quiet," said the green genie.
"That's what I want!" said the blue genie. "But I know I
can't make my own wish come true."

"But *I* can!" said the green genie. "I can wish for you, and you can wish for me." Then he puffed himself up and said . . .

"ABC and XYZ,
Broccoli broth and breakfast in bed."

He rubbed his tummy and patted his head,
and the teapot grew a pair of wings.

"Jump in! Let's go!" said the green genie.
The teapot carried the two genies out of the farmhouse,
away from the farm, over the hills and through the clouds.

Then it came gently down to rest on a beautiful beach.
The only sound was the lapping of the waves on the shore.
The two genies had a little paddle.

Then the green genie wished for another teapot and some teacups and the blue genie made that wish come true.

After their cup of tea, the two genies
climbed into the first teapot
and fell asleep.

Please don't disturb them if you ever find that teapot on the beach. Or if you really feel you have to, just make one wish. Think very hard:

what will that wish be?

For Rita – J.D.

For Jasmine, Salima and Bella and all the cousins, with love – A.C.

First published 2020 by Macmillan Children's Books
This edition published 2021 by Macmillan Children's Books
an imprint of Pan Macmillan
The Smithson, 6 Briset Street, London EC1M 5NR
EU representative: Macmillan Publishers Ireland Limited
1st Floor, The Liffey Trust Centre, 117-126 Sheriff Street Upper
Dublin 1, D01 YC43
Associated companies throughout the world.
www.panmacmillan.com

ISBN: 978-1-5098-4359-6

3 5 7 9 8 6 4 2

A CIP catalogue record for this book is available from the British Library.

Printed in Spain.